Phoebe and Her Unicorn in

The Magic Storm

Phoebe and Her Unicorn in

The Magic Storm

Dana Simpson

PHOEBE!
On it.
sploosh
Thank you!

It's been a while since I had to rescue you from gazing at your reflection.
I have gotten much better!
In times of stress and anxiety, we fall back on old habits.
What're you anxious about?
I am not sure.

But the magical frequencies are buzzing MOST OMINOUSLY. They are telling me that disturbing forces are at work.
I think you're right.
Phoebe! You have acquired magic sensitivity?
No, I just got an extreme weather warning on my phone.
Should we continue on to your school?
It doesn't say school is canceled. I think I still have to go.

If you should need me, you can summon me with the UNICORN SUMMONING DANCE.
I'll just text you. That video Dakota took of me doing the Unicorn Summoning Dance got two million views.
Heeey losers.
Speaking of Dakota.

How come you still call me that? I ride a UNICORN to school now.
And I actually AM a unicorn.
I think you're JEALOUS.
Of YOU? For THAT? Psh.
I was making fun of you for being a loser LONG before the unicorn showed up.
You were...jealous for some other reason, then!

Besides, yeah, you sit on a pointy horse. Big whoop.
To THESE things, I'm a QUEEN or something.
BLART
"Or something"?
BLAAAAART
Can YOU understand them?
BLART

But they carry me to and from school on this...throne thingy, so...
MARIGOLD is my throne thingy.
Yes, I am Phoebe's throne thingy.
Nice try, but we all know being the QUEEN of ANYTHING is better than just sitting on some HORN-HORSE.
BLART.
Yeah, well...we'll race you to school!
No way. I know your horse thingy is FASTER.

But I'm gonna get there with more STYLE.
I think you may be overestimating how stylish goblins are.
You are DEFINITELY underestimating the stylishness of unicorns.
blart
What he said.
See you at school.

TIPTON ELEMENTARY
SCHOOL BUS
I will not go far, in case school is canceled and you need a ride.
Stay warm!
My magical Shield of Warmingness will protect me!

EXIT
Did you hear? An ice storm is coming!
I heard they might have to end school early today!

Hey, kids. Seems like we have a lot of absences.
And looking outside, I dunno how long we're actually gonna BE here.
So...here. Have a film.
This is the story of how they make masking tape.
It all begins with the
Psst. Give this to Phoebe.
of paper

an easily-released, pressure-sensitive adhesive
wind it into rolls
PHOEBE STINKS
and then you use it to like, hang posters

used it
Give this to Dakota.
pair of glasses together when
also be used for marking off areas for paint
blart
blart
blart
mud
you
has a lower tack, s

decorative Japanese washi masking tape
I am a stupid horn-horse
I personally like your unicorn better. A goblin broke my phone, and she fixed it. —MAX

Meanwhile...
WHAM!
Are you all right?
Mmf. Seems so.

I have never seen a pixie collide with a tree before.
Don't rub it in.
Do Pixies not fly based on magical GPS?
My antennae aren't getting a signal.
Will you be all right?
It's fine. I'll just have to look where I'm going.

Hm. I have very poor magic reception out here!
Only one bar! I will not be able to get or send magical text messages.
Something besides bad weather is ahoof.
I must go and make sure Phoebe is all right!

Attention, teachers and students...that freezing rain is really coming down out there, and the roads aren't gonna be safe for long.
We're calling a half day. You can meet the buses outside.
"Freezing rain." That's weird. Why isn't it just snow? Or hail?
It has to do with where the air is cold and where it isn't.
If it's above freezing up where the cloud is, but below freezing down closer to the ground, the rain freezes, and you get what's happening now.

It's cool that you know stuff like that.
It's cool that stuff like that HAPPENS.
I dunno. It's pretty inconvenient.
Maybe, but I can't stay mad at weather. I love it too much.
Stay safe, Max.
You too, Phoebe.

Zuh. Why don't you two just KISS, already?
Why do you hafta be so mean, Dakota?
I'm not mean!
You make fun of me all the time.
You MAKE me make fun of you by being weird.
If you would just be COOL, I wouldn't HAVE to make fun of you.

I AM SO cool.
Name one way you're cool.
I can play the piano!
That's not cool.
I can beat the game "Portable Hole" without dying!
Totally not helping your case.
I have, um, this hat.
Mm hmm.
Do I have to mention the unicorn again?

You get carried around by goblins. How am I the weird one?
I know. It's totally amazing! And yet here we are.
You know what? Maybe I don't CARE what you think.
Maybe you're a big mean stupidface and I'm actually way cooler than you will EVER be.
Mm.
Mm.

Stay safe, Dakota.
You too I guess.
We must get you home. I fear it is worse than I had thought!

The air is colder down here than it is up higher.
Max says that's how ice storms happen.
What?
Perhaps something on the ground is... STEALING the heat.
Likely, whatever is stealing the ambient magic in this area.

What could be doing THAT?
I do not know.
I will drop you off at your house, and then I will investigate further.
Okay, but...
You have to promise to stay safe.
And you have to come back to my house as soon as you're done, to get warm.

Worsening weather, and now I have no magic reception at all!
I cannot get ANY channels on magic satellite radio.
I will go somewhere high and see if that helps.

No...it is no better up here.
Lovely view, though.
I do hope Phoebe is all right.

I hope Marigold is all right.

DING-DONG
Marigold! Come in and get warm.
It is not just that I am cold... I am feeling a different kind of chill.

The normal background magic has gone out ENTIRELY. It is very disturbing.
I am sparkling as hard as I can right now! And as you can see, nothing!
So...would you say you SENSE A GREAT DISTURBANCE IN THE FORCE?
I would not say that.
PLEASE say that!

I refuse.
Spoilsport.
Heyyyyy, losers. Welcome to SoDakota.
If you and Dakota are not friends, why do you watch her vlog?
It's complicated.
This is a special ice storm edition. It's, like, seriously cold.

I gotta say, I wasn't sure about these goblin things at first.
They didn't make a good first impression.
BLART
BLART
Didn't help that the first time I met them, they abducted me to an abandoned burger joint so they could steal the enchantment from my hair.
(For more on that, go watch SoDakota #48.)
But now they treat me as their princess or queen or SOMETHING special, for some reason. And you DO get used to the smell.
And they give off SOOO much heat! Which is awesome when it's so cold outside.

Can YOU emit heat?
Normally, yes.
When the magic is not down, I can emit as much heat as I wish with my magical SHIELD of WARMINGNESS!
plink
I can usually also emit LIGHT. That would be useful right now.

AAAAAA!
That's dad's way of saying the Internet is out.
NO NO NO NO NO NO NOOOO!
The horror...
Maybe it's a good thing if you unplug for a bit, love.
This is a SERIOUS STORM!

This is more than a storm.
This is a MYSTERY. Of a MAGICAL sort.
It's a job for the PHOEBEGOLD DETECTIVE AGENCY!
Tomorrow, we shall investigate.
For now, we should get comfortable.

HA!

You landed on my hotel! You owe me THOUSAND DOLLARS!
Mm. I don't HAVE that much.
Yessss!
So...I basically WIN, right?
Yeah, you've pretty much won.

But the game isn't over?
Oh, not even close.
It's going to drag on for another few hours, while we start mortgaging everything and you bleed us dry.
Why?
Because it's a boring, Internetless wasteland, and our options are pretty limited.
ptoo

It's Phoebe's bedtime anyway.
Aw.
Aw.
Alas.
If you go to sleep now, there's a pretty good chance the power'll be back on when you wake up.
I wish Marigold could be my night-light.
Then I have good news!

How? You said the magic is out.
I have been SAVING some.
We'll play "Pioneers of Palash" by firelight. It'll be super romantic.
Being married to you is the BEST.
SAVING some?
I have an emergency backup store of magic.
I knew it would be JUST ENOUGH for night-light purposes.

Mm. Good morning, Phoebe.
Morning, Marigold... magic still out?
I fear so.
Morning, kiddo and unicorn. Have some cereal.

The milk's okay?
It got cold in here after we turned off the fireplace last night.
Your mom and I are gonna pass the time by playing poker for M&Ms. You two in?

Actually, I was hoping Phoebe would come outside with me, to investigate.
The fact that the magic is out, as well as the electricity, makes me suspect this is more than a mere ice storm.
Well, wrap up warm!
And don't be gone too long. It's chilly out there.

Without magic, the world feels very strange.

What's it feel like?
It feels like...
You know how sometimes your foot is asleep?
Your horn is asleep?
It is quite upsetting.

Wow, it seems like the power's out everywhere.
Not everywhere.
DRAGON'S DEN COMICS
Why there?
I do not know. Curious.

The snow's starting to stick.
That, I do not find upsetting.
I am hoping it will help conceal me!
THE PRANCING PONY
JOE'S
Because...I am feeling a bit conspicuous.

No magic means no Shield of Boringness.
U-unicorn.
Good thing the weather's terrible, or there'd be even more people out here staring.
Although, you know...
I kinda like it. When people gaze at YOU in wonderment, they see ME, too.

BEHOLD ME, WORLD! I AM PHOEBE, UNICORN RIDER!!!

Don't tell me you don't kinda enjoy it, too. I see you. I see how you're prancing.
WOOOW.
Perhaps a bit.
It is the unicorn dilemma. We want to be left alone...but we love being the center of attention.
It has been nice for a little while.

But getting to the bottom of this may require us to be inconspicuous.
And what is the first rule of the PHOEBEGOLD DETECTIVE AGENCY?
Disguises are fun!
Precisely!
Tipton Costumes
Because Disguises R Fun
412

Costumes
The lady just said "unicorns are so beautiful," so I don't think it's stealing.
There are never enough four-legged costume options.
Does it seem like people are only staring at us MORE?

Perhaps we should get away from downtown.
Still, that was a fun costuming interlude.
Oh, entirely worth it, yes.
City of Tipton
HILLCREST PARK

Perhaps from a high place such as this, I can get a better sense of where the magic blockage is.
Hrm. Nothing.
You two are up here trying to avoid the gawkers too, huh?

Oh...hey, Dakota.
Saw you guys down there. You look weird.
But it seems like you're having the same problems we are.
blart

I am not surprised. Like unicorns, goblins depend on the power of magic to avoid human stares.
Goblins use the Shield of Boringness?
Something like that.
Their version is known as the *Bubble of Non-Grossness.*

I HAVE been noticing the smell more than usual.
BLART.
He says the feeling is mutual.
You speak Goblin?
I get by.

We have more important things to worry about.
I agree, actually.
So we'll talk about your outfit later.
Blart blart
Blart.
The power's out, the Internet is out...
It's seriously inconveniencing me.
Blart blart blart.

I had to wash my hair in cold water, and then I couldn't dry it.
So that's why it hasn't changed position since we've been here.
Frozen solid. It's like having aluminum hair.
Blart?
BLART BLART BLAART.
plink plink plink

What are you guys TALKING about over there?
Many things.
She has been remarking on my thick unicorn accent.
Blart.
He likes the video game Portable Hole 3.
Blart blart.

And HE thinks the TV show "Pastel Unicorns" has been going downhill for a few seasons.
blart
Now, SHE is remarking that the new album by Blart and the Blarts is groundbreaking.
Have they said anything relevant to the current situation?
One thing.
It is an ANCIENT GOBLIN LEGEND.

Is this really the time for stories?
It may well be. For this is...
The Legend of Voltina, the Dragon of Electricity and Magic.
Once upon a time, there was a goblin town on a vast plain.

And on a nearby hilltop there lived a dragon.

Her name was Voltina, and she was the sort of dragon who ATE LIGHTNING!

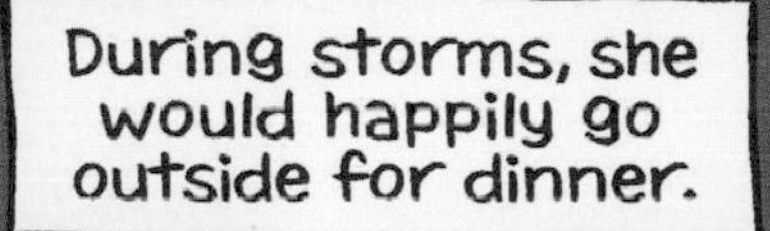
During storms, she would happily go outside for dinner.

And for a long time, she lived contentedly that way.

And the goblins mostly ignored her, and went about their usual goblin business.
blart
blart
But then one day there was a particularly terrible lightning storm, and the goblins finally noticed she was there!
BLART!
BLART!
And they marched to the mountain, and accused her of CAUSING the storm.
blart
blart
blart

It was not a very productive conversation, so nothing immediately came of it.
Blart!
Blart!
...what?
But she got the gist of it, and it gave her ideas.
She began to research weather magic, learning how to cause storms.

And it was not long before she could cause some truly fearsome storms!

And when that was not enough, she learned to eat the heat out of the atmosphere, causing the weather to grow very cold.

This all made her very unpopular with the goblins in the town.
How uncouth!
And because weather spells are so magic-intensive, she was using up all the magic in the area, annoying the local unicorns.
BLART!
Indeed!
The goblins and unicorns got together to decide what to do about the situation.

And so they chased her away.
With, like, torches and pitchforks?
Those do not work on dragons.
What does?
A STERNLY WORDED PETITION.

How long ago did this happen, according to the legend?
Blart blart!
They say it was SEVEN HUNDRED YEARS ago.
Or last Tuesday. Goblins are not great with time.
Blart.
Do you think that's actually REAL?

It is as good an explanation as I can think of.
Okay, so if we believe the goblins, which is a pretty big "if"...
What do we do?
Yeah. Where would we FIND her?

Blart blart BLAAART blart!
What's he saying?
He suggests we wait for the next lightning strike. She almost certainly will be under it.
So we have to predict lightning? Fantastic.
It looks like the power's out all over town. Does that tell us anything?

I do not know enough about how your electricity works.
Me neither.
Or me.
BLART.
What we need now is a REAL NERD.
Wait. Are you saying I'm NOT a nerd?

Oh, you are definitely a GIGANTIC nerd.
Dang right.
But we need the right KIND of nerd. Someone who knows how stuff works.
I know someone like that!
Right, your weird friend?

Glasses boy.
Max.
Right, him.
poke
sigh
poke
poke
poke
poke
poke
poke
poke
siiiiigh
poke
poke
poke
poke
poke
poke
poke

Max?
Your friend Phoebe and another girl are here.
Be there in a minute, mom.
Your tablet's not suddenly going to start working.
You don't know that.

Your one friend is downstairs, Max. You should let her distract you.
Besides, we need you.
Need me for what?
Your other mother is... stuck.
Stuck how?
Just come on.

This is why we need the Shield of Boringness.
...unicorn.
Hey, Phoebe. Unicorn. Dakota. Little green guys.

Hey, Max...
If you wanted to eat the electricity for the entire town, where would you go?
What?
Humor me.
Well...you would need a map of the power lines and substations to figure that out.

Great, I bet we could find that online!
...oh, right, Phone's dead and wi-fi is down.
I know. It's tearing me apart.
Fortunately, I have one in my room.
You have a map of the electrical grid in your room?
I did a science fair project on it.

I remember that. That was pretty cool!
You have a strange definition of "cool."
That's a lot of potatoes.
For THIS year's science fair, I'm making a giant potato battery.
Can we hurry this up? I'm getting nerd contamination.

Here we go. I hand-drew this map myself.
That's a TON of detail.
It combines two things I love: electricity and maps.
Here. This power station. It's not far.

Great. Can you write down some directions for us?
Directions? I'm obviously coming with you.
Yeah. I mean, I was gonna just poke uselessly at my phone all day, but I can reschedule that.
Really?
Yeah, probably.
BLART.

Okay, but I have to warn you...
There may be a DRAGON involved.
You really should have LED with that.
Then I have to warn you there may NOT be a dragon involved.

Unicorn.
I know, right?
Now both your moms are stuck staring at Marigold.
Yeah, we should get going.

Hang on just a sec.
Hey, Marigold...I've been wondering something.
Yes, Phoebe?
With the *Shield of Boringness* down, Max's parents were, like, dumbstruck by your magnificence and whatever.
Yes!

But Max and Dakota aren't.
They have spent time around me.
One can become accustomed to almost anything.

Even a unicorn.
I guess that's true. It happened to me so gradually I didn't really notice.
When I first saw you, you were the most amazing thing I'd ever seen.
Now I see you all the time and you're my best frienc
Which I LOVE, but it's a lot more...normal.

Is that bad?
I dunno. It's just new.
On reflection, I prefer it.
So I guess we should go solve this mystery.
That, too, will be new!

I'll need a ride from one of you guys.
BLART
BLART.
The goblins say they will only carry Dakota

Blart.
Darn right.
So I suppose it will have to be me!
Thanks.
It must be nice, having a friend you can ride.

Marigold is neat for a lot of other reasons.
It is true! We share many interests.
Such as UNICORNS!
Yeah, but not JUST unicorns.

Like, we read books together... sometimes we play video games...
And I love long walks as much as Phoebe does!
And Dakota and the goblins are all into... um...
Dakota, I guess.
Blart.

We have other stuff in common.
These guys REALLY like to watch "Pretty High School Kids Having Feelings" with me.
Blart.
But, it also makes sense goblins would gravitate to her. They are a matriarchal society.
So they appreciate a certain kind of assertive, confident–
The word you're looking for is "bossy."

And it's true. Bossy girls get ALL the goblins.
Blart.
Any of you into "Space Journey"? Or, well, stuff like the town electrical grid?
I find those things moderately interesting.
I get why you like them. I think it's COOL that you like them.

Yeah...
that's usually
the best I
can hope for.
Whoa.
There
it is.

Weird that we didn't notice that towering storm cloud.
Well, there are a lot of tall trees here.

DANGER
HIGH VOLTAGE
Huh. It's not locked.
There is a version of the legend in which Voltina is also a skilled locksmith
You didn't mention that earlier.
I did not know it would be relevant.

You should not go any further. It would be unsafe.
Suits me, but...
I sense a concealment spell at work.
I shall employ the last of my backup magic.
How come I don't see anything?

Oh magic sparkles, now I sing For you to show the hidden thing! We wish to see what's missing here So make what's now concealed appear!
Since when do your magic spells require you to sing about them?
Since I decided to start adding FLAIR.
Hey. Nerds.
Look.

She has the same sadness in her eyes the legend describes.
Between that and the locksmi thing, I feel lik you left a lot o details out of this legend.
I have trouble keeping track of details that are not about me.
So...what do we do?
Blart
BLART.
BLAAART.
Blart

Blart!
Blart blart.
BLART.
BLART
blart
BLART
Blart!
Blart blart blart!!

BLART.
Blart.
BLART.
Blart!
BLÄRT.
BLAAAAART.
BLART.

BLART.
Hmph.

I actually do not blame her. The goblins made a singularly unpersuasive argument.
Step aside, losers. I'll handle this.

Look at me. I'm WAY cooler than you are. So you should do what I say.
And I say, "get out of here, you voltage-slurping weirdo."
Why are you here anyway? Nobody WANTS you here.
Eating all the electricity totally messes everything up. We'd ALL be happier if you'd just GO AWAY and leave us ALONE.

You are the LEAST POPULAR PERSON HERE. I'm way too cool to even be SEEN with you.
SO GO ON! GET OUT OF HERE!
Sigh
I don't get it. That's worked with like ten kids at school.
You're a monster, Dakota.

I will go next.
Voltina...assuming you ARE the Voltina of legend...
You are using up all the local ambient magic, and that is very inconvenient for me!
I am sure you can tell by glancing at me that I am magnificent, and you can therefore understand that I am too magnificent for the unprotected human gaze.

I want to be able to walk among them without inspiring constant gape-mouthed awe. And it would be a terrible tragedy for a unicorn not to get what she wants!
I like Phoebe, and I would not want my shimmering beauty to interfere with the two of us hanging out
That sounds lovely.

Why is none of this working?
The legend s unclear on hat worked, but it is lear nothing bvious did.
Well, then what would?

What if we find out what music she really hates, and play it as loud as we can?
Or maybe we could find out what kind of food she likes, and lure her outside the switching station with the smell of it?
BLART.
What if we all got air horns and blew them really loud?
We could get earplugs, so we don't-
I...think I know what's happening here.

You do?
I recognize it. I've done it myself!
She's COMFORT EATING.
You think?
Remember the spelling bee last year?

Do I! That was hi-*LAR*-ious.
You lost on the word "triumph."
It haunts me to this day.
As I recall, you ate an entire bucket of ice cream.
As I recall, I got pretty sick.

I also do recall you making precisely that expression.
Excuse me...Miz Voltina?

I think I know what's going on.
Are you sad?
You can talk about it if you want.
I'm lonely.

You see, once upon a time, I lived on a hilltop, near a goblin town.
blart
blart
And I would feast on the lightning any time there was a storm.
Oo, yum!

And for a long time, I was mostly okay.

Um, excuse me...
But my attempts to be friends with the goblins didn't seem to go particularly well.
Blart
Blart
Blart
Partly, there was a language barrier.
BLART.
Could you repeat that?
t's hard to make friends vhen you can't explain yourself.

Every time I fed on a storm, the goblins looked at me with more distrust.
What?
Next I tried to be friends with local unicorns.
Um, hello.

But they paid little mind.
TRA LA LA WE ARE SO BEAUTIFUL
I was lonely and depressed.
BAT-R-E
So I started eating more.

So you ate the heat from the air, and it got cold!
I did not.
The LEGEND says you did.
It was cold. It was JANUARY.
I guess that is legends for you.

Often there were not enough storms for me to eat my fill.
So I began to learn the magic craft of creating my OWN storms.
And soon, I was causing storms every day.

This made me even less popular with the goblins.
NO
BLART
DARGN = BAD
And because weather spells are magic-intensive, I was using up all the local ambient magic!
How UNCOUTH!
This annoyed the unicorns.
So I had no friends at all.
And that only made me hungrier.

So then the goblins gave you a strongly worded petition!
What?
The legend says-
I don't know where you're getting this information.
No, they just chased me with brooms.

After the fourth or fifth time they did that, I decided I shouldn't stay where I wasn't wanted.
That's...that's awful. I'm so sorry.
And I wandered the earth, until I found this place.
By then I was quite hungry, not having eaten in several hours.
Wait, hours

Yes. All of this happened yesterday.
So kind of a recent legend, then.
And since clearly no one wants me here either...
Actually...

I want you here.

You do?
Yeah. You're the first person I've met who's as interested in electrical grids as me!
ve tried to et Phoebe nterested.
It's true! I gave it a shot, but... nope.
I never even tried with Dakota.
That was smart.
Maybe you'd ke to see my capacitor collection?
Would I!

And, um...
maybe you'd
like to see the
potato battery
I'm making!
Please.
Take me to
this wondrous
thing.
I believe
we have
achieved the
objective of
our quest.
Yeah...maybe
we should get
out of here!

I'm hungry.
Yes, a successful quest does whet the appetite!
Let's go into town and get lunch.
What do you say, Voltina? Wanna join us for lunch?
Really?
Maybe you could give Max a lift.

I will tag along, but if it is all the same, I do not believe I will eat anything.
I am, finally, full.

So hey, after that, you wanna come over to my house? I have a video game you might like..."Dr. Shock vs. the Electro Men."
What is a video game?
Oh, man. This is gonna be fun.

THREE MONTHS LATER
TIPTON ELEMENTARY
Nice day, huh?
Any day we get to do this is nice.

You said something a little while back about how you can get used to anything, even unicorns.
That sounds like me.
Yeah, well...
I'm not tired of this yet.
Nor am I.

And I do like spring. The new leaves...the smell of flowers...
And that.
Heyyyyy, you guys.
So where are Max and his ride?

Here we are!
We were almost late! Voltina and I were having a marathon Dr. Shock" tournament.

I won!
Also, the electricity at Max's house is delicious. It is hard sometimes to tear myself away.
It must be expensive.
Oh, terribly.

It is a good thing that, like all dragons, I have an extensive golden hoard to compensate them for it!
And she eats a lot less of it now than when we met her.
I am getting a magic text message!
Who's it from?
Oh, a unicorn magic alert system to which I subscribe.

It seems that a group of singing pixies is headed in the general direction of town.
Cool!
Would tha it were s
Pixie songs have been known to drive mortals MAD.

I propose our little group put in some magic earplugs and go save the town again.
No offense, Voltina.
None taken! It was all just a mis-understanding.
Sure, I'm in.
Me too.
Yeah, why not, it'll give me something to vlog about.
BLART.

Voltina, do you know how to stop Pixies?
Seems like asking nicely would be a place to start.
So I guess now the Phoebegold Detective Agency has a lot more members.
What about Phoebmarigobdakmaxtina?
If this group has a name, there's no way it's that.
Hey unicorn, about those magic earplugs.

MAX'S GUIDE TO POWER PLANTS

Ever wondered where the electricity in your house comes from? It all starts at a power plant—also called a "power station." Here's how the power gets to you.

Fuel (like coal or natural gas) is burned in a giant **furnace**.

The heat from the furnace flows up into a **boiler**, heating the water pipes until a flow of steam is produced.

The pressure from the passing steam turns the metal blades of the **turbine** wheel. The hot steam is condensed and moved through the **cooling tower** so that it turns back into water and can be reused.

The turbine is attached to a **generator**, which uses the motion from the turbine to make electricity. When the turbine is in motion, the wires inside a magnetic field within the generator turn, creating electricity.

The electricity travels out of the generator through **energy cables** to a nearby **step-up transformer** that boosts the electricity to a very high voltage so it can be carried over long distances.

Tall metal **transmission towers** carry the electricity through energy cables to wherever it's needed.

Once the electricity reaches its destination, it goes through a **step-down transformer** that converts it to a lower voltage that can be used in your home after it passes through underground cables to reach the wall **outlets** in your house.

WHAT ACTUALLY CAUSES POWER OUTAGES?

Are magical storms really to blame when the power goes out? Here's what's behind blackouts:

- **Trees**: If they're not properly pruned, sometimes trees can grow too big or weaken with age, and they interfere with power lines.
- **Storms**: Strong winds, lightning, flooding, and ice can also weaken trees and increases the chances of them falling on electrical equipment. If a storm is strong enough, it can even knock down poles or power lines on its own!
- **Wildlife**: Believe it or not, but dragons only account for a tiny percentage of power outages—other animals such as squirrels, snakes, and birds are more often to blame for damage because they are attracted to the warmth of the electrical equipment or in search of food in electrical substations.
- **Equipment failure**: The electrical grid is very complicated, and sometimes equipment can fail due to age. Other times, equipment fails because it's unable to handle high demand—for example, when everyone in a big city has the air-conditioning on high during an unusually hot summer day.
- **Miscellaneous damage**: What happens if a car crashes into a utility pole? Or what if construction equipment damages power lines? There are many other unusual ways in which the electrical grid can be damaged.

DRINKABLE BLUE LIGHTNING

The drink of dragons! You'll need a black light to experience the full effect of this electrifying drink. The secret is the quinine found in tonic water, which glows in the dark when exposed to a black light.

INGREDIENTS:
water
tonic water, regular or diet
powdered lemonade drink mix

Fill 1/3 of your glass with water, and fill the rest of the glass with tonic water. Add powdered lemonade to taste and mix it well. Then turn out the lights, flip on your black light, and enjoy the zinging, bubbly power of blue lightning in a glass.

WATER-BENDING MAGIC TRICK

You'll think you're wielding magic with this science experiment that relies on static electricity. Shock your friends with a trick that they'll have to see to believe.

TOOLS YOU NEED

nylon comb
water tap (such as the faucet in your kitchen sink)

INSTRUCTIONS

1. Slowly turn on the water tap until you get a small stream of water—the smaller the better, as long as it's a complete stream and not a trickle of drops.
2. Run the comb through your dry hair at least fifteen times. This will charge the plastic with static electricity.
3. Move the comb toward the stream of water without touching it. Go slowly, and behold the power of static electricity!

GLOSSARY

ambient (am-bee-ent): pg. 29 – adjective / relating to the immediate surroundings; usually used to describe things like light, temperature, sound, etc.

capacitor (ca-pass-it-ter): pg. 139 – noun / a device used to store electrical energy

golden hoard (gold-en hord): pg. 149 – noun / a huge collection of gold hat's been stored somewhere, usually hidden away

gravitate (grav-i-tate): pg. 104 – verb / to move toward something as f pulled by an unseen force

nconspicuous (in-con-spic-u-us): pg. 58 – adjective / not immediately noticeable

ocksmith (lock-smith): pg. 108 – noun / a person who makes or repairs ocks

natriarchal (may-tree-ark-al): pg. 104 – adjective / describing a society n which women are the leaders

mortgaging (mort-gij-ing): pg. 43 – verb / give someone legal claim to a piece of property you own in exchange for money to be paid back over ime

ominously (om-in-nus-lee): pg. 8 – adverb / happening in a way that suggests something bad is going to happen

relevant (rel-lev-vent): pg. 108 – adjective / closely connected to what s being done or considered

ingularly (sin-gew-lar-lee): pg. 116 – adjective / in a remarkable or xtraordinary way

ubstations (sub-stay-shuns): pg. 89 – noun / secondary power stations where electric current is transformed so that it can be supplied to customers

ncouth (un-cooth): pg. 78 – adjective / lacking polish or grace

Andrews McMeel Publishing
a division of Andrews McMeel Universal
1130 Walnut Street, Kansas City, Missouri 64106

www.andrewsmcmeel.com

17 18 19 20 21 SDB 10 9 8 7 6 5 4 3 2 1

ISBN: 978-1-4494-8359-3

Library of Congress Control Number: 2017931089

Made by:
Shenzhen Donnelley Printing Company Ltd.
Address and location of manufacturer:
No. 47, Wuhe Nan Road, Bantian Ind. Zone,
Shenzhen China, 518129
1st Printing—7/24/17

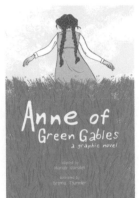

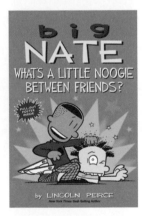

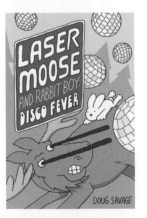